OTHER NOVELS BY HARRY KATZAN, JR.
A Matt, the General and Ashley Series

Life is Good

Everything is Good

The Last Adventure

The Romeo Affair

Another Romeo Affair

We Can Only Hope for It

EVERYTHING IS ALL RIGHT

Harry Katzan Jr.

 iUniverse

EVERYTHING IS ALL RIGHT

iUniverse books may be ordered through booksellers or by contacting:

iUniverse
1663 Liberty Drive
Bloomington, IN 47403
www.iuniverse.com
844-349-9409

ISBN: 978-1-6632-5403-0 (sc)
ISBN: 978-1-6632-5405-4 (hc)
ISBN: 978-1-6632-5404-7 (e)

Library of Congress Control Number: 2023911536

Print information available on the last page.

iUniverse rev. date: 06/16/2023

For Margaret, my best girl now and forever
With all my love

CONTENTS

Part 6: Back to Normal

INTRODUCTION

This novel, as in the previous sixteen stories in the series involving Matt, the General, and Ashley, and the assistance of their associates and friends, Matt, the General, and Ashley combine their efforts to solve important problems that involve the United States, foreign countries, and personal safety in the domestic area. In this instance, the book is set in the beautiful area of middle New Jersey in the United States.

As in the previous novels, Matt Miller, who has a PhD from a prestigious university, uses his mathematical thinking and solid logic, along with the organizational ability of General Les Miller, his grandfather, and the common sense and clear thinking of Ashley Miller, Matt's wife to solve some personal situations of friends and associates. Matt takes advantage of an old school friend Harp Thomas, who is a professor in Switzerland to sort out some important issues relating to family matters.

In the cases covered herein, the team tried to solve problems and mitigate issues that many of us face in everyday lives. The problems are vexing and the solutions are intended to give the reader a good feeling that everything is really all right. However, this is a not a book with an abundance of words and little thought. This is an important book for all of us.

As with all of the author's books, there is no violence, no sex, and no bad language and is accessible to persons of all ages.

I hope you enjoy reading this book as much as I enjoyed writing it. Thank you for purchasing it.

The author,
July, 2023

MAIN CHARACTERS
IN THE BOOK

The General – Les Miller. Former military General and Humanitarian. P-51 pilot and World War II hero.

Matthew (Matt) Miller – Professor of Mathematics. Grandson of the General. Sophisticated problem solver and strategist.

Ashley Wilson Miller – College friend of Matt Miller. Former Duchess of Bordeaux. Married to Matt Miller. Is a Receiver of the National Medal of Freedom.

Marguerite Purgoine – Retired creative writing Professor and an associate of the team. Known as Anna for some unknown reason. Wife of the General.

Betty Roberts - The General's housekeeper trained at Le Cordon Bleu with a Master's degree. Exceedingly intelligent.

General Clark - Mark Clark. Former Four Star General and Chairman of the Joint Chiefs of Staff. Appointed to be U.S. Director of Intelligence.

Kimberly Scott – The Intelligence specialist of the U.S.

Harry Steevens – Expert mathematician and former college friend of Matt Miller. Policeman in New Jersey.

Katherine Penelope Radford – Retired Queen of the United Kingdom and personal friend of the General.

Harp Thomas – Academic friend of Matt and professor of mathematics at ETH Zürich Switzerland.

Gregory Kacan – Matt's and Harp's thesis advisor. Retired professor.

Katarina Kacan – Gregory's wife. Deceased in the story.

Dr. Hutchinson - Military psychiatrist and project leader.

END OF CHARACTERS

PART 1

*Meeting the Characters
in the Story*

CHAPTER 1

WHAT DO YOU DO WHEN IT IS RAINING

Matt awakened Ashley with a steaming hot mug of coffee. All he said was, "good morning sweetie. It is raining."

"My goodness," said Ashley, half-awake. "It's 6 am. It's too early to get up. Did the General call again? I didn't hear it. Thanks for the coffee, but you might–as–well drink it yourself. I'm going back to sleep; weren't we going to Starbucks today?"

Like clock work, the phone rang and they knew it had to be the General. Only he called at this time of the night or the morning, depending upon who you asked.

"Hello," said Matt. "Why are you calling at 6am, when it's raining and we can't play a round of golf this morning?"

"What do you think we should do?" asked the General. "I know you have work to do with that string theory, but we could do something for a couple of hours. Anyway, you should be writing books and not reading them."

"It's easy to read a book," said Ashley. "Just read the first chapter and the last chapter and hope that no one asks you about the insides. Do you know that in prize-winning novels, the first and last chapters are the shortest."

"You just made that up," said the General. "But I get the point. Some of these characters get on TV and say they read 300 books in a year, and here is what you should read."

Ashley whispered to Matt, "8 o'clock at Starbucks."

"Ashley has a good idea," said Matt. "Can you meet us at Starbucks at 8 o'clock. They have good breakfast sandwiches."

"Is it alright if I bring my housekeeper?" asked the General.

"Is she your new girl friend?" asked Ashley with a sly smile.

Mat elbowed her, and put his finger to his lips, as if to say 'stop it'.

"Of course not," said the General. "You know me better than that. "She had a tough time when I was on that temporary military duty, and she did a good job, and she needs someone to be nice to her once in a while."

"We would love to have her," said Matt. "What does she do for you, anyway?"

"Listen," said the General. "She's a manager: she has a cook every day, a fat cleaning lady 4 times a week, a thin lady twice a week, a gardener 5 days a week, and she takes care of my accountant. And she answers the door. So there."

"We'll see the two of you, General," said Ashley apologetically. "Drive carefully. Take your pills with orange juice before you leave."

"I don't take any pills," said the General. "I'll see you at 8. By the way, this housekeeper of mine has a Master's degree."

END OF CHAPTER ONE

CHAPTER 2

BREAKFAST AT STARBUCKS

On the way to Starbucks, Matt and Ashley were deep in conversation.

"How could that housekeeper have a Master's degree?" asked Ashley.

"I don't have a clue," said Matt. "But, when I first met you, I told you that the General brought a European golf champion and his wife and kids to teach me how to play golf. It was 6 weeks and then he paid for their vacation in the U.S. He might just want his employees to be the best they can be. I think this breakfast will be interesting."

"Does the General drink much alcohol?" asked Ashley. "All I've seen him drink is that single malt scotch and eat his prime filet. What is this single malt scotch business?"

"I just don't know," said Matt. "He must have drunk beer when he was in the Army. Especially for pilots who might get killed in the next mission. Come to think of it, have you seen him drink coffee? The single malt scotch is the product of only one brewery. They usually mix the scotch drink from several breweries to achieve a special taste, like they do in France with that Bordeaux wine."

"Not that I can remember," said Ashley. "That is about coffee you just mentioned. That guy that replaced our air conditioning only drank water. When I asked them if they wanted a soda or something, he said he only drank water and never did drink anything else - no alcohol, no coffee or tea, no soda, and no fruit juice - for his whole life. His father was the same way. He looks pretty young and has a daughter that graduated from college."

"And his partner, who must have drunk and eaten both shares, " replied Matt. "He was so fat that he fell asleep on our porch when he should have been working."

"We should ask the General what he thinks about drinking," continued Ashley. "I mean about drinking in general. It could be interesting. What are you going to have to eat?"

"I guess I'll have the breakfast sandwich - there are several varieties - and those string like potatoes, and coffee," said Matt. "I don't want to look too cheap and just have a sandwich. I'll pay this time. I don't have any charges on my credit card, and they will probably close me down if I go too long without making a charge, I haven't made a charge in almost a year."

"Look ahead," exclaimed Ashley. There is your grandfather, right in front of Starbucks getting out of his car. He's opening the door for her. What's her name?"

"Betty," answered Matt.

Matt parked next to the General, and Ashley was the first to speak.

"You're in a no parking zone, General," said Ashley with a smile on her face. "You will get a ticket."

"I'm not parking," said the General. "If I were parking, I would be over there in the parking area. I'm not there, so I am not parking."

"Then, what are you doing?" asked Betty, the housekeeper. "Looks like you're parking to me."

"Okay, everyone thinks I'm parking, but I am not," said the General. "And the police or whomever will agree with me. Doesn't matter, if I get a ticket, Matt will pay."

So the four of them walked into Starbucks and everyone stopped working.

"What's happening?" asked the Manager.

"Just look," said a worker. "Those high-classed people that just walked in."

"Well, I'll be," said the Manager. He was totally uninterested.

It was an enjoyable breakfast. Everyone had the same: breakfast sandwich, potatoes, and a Grandi coffee, except the General, who had water.

"Don't you ever drink coffee or tea, Mr. Miller?" asked Betty.

"Never do and never did," said the General. "I used to drink beer with the other pilots – it was 3% beer – and haven't drink beer anymore after I was promoted to Captain. I do drink single malt scotch when I have dinner, which is prime filet. I drank beer with the other pilots, because we were afraid of dying in combat."

"How many times were you promoted?" asked Ashley referring to the General..

"He won't answer," said Matt. "I'll list them after Captain and Major that is skipped because in war time, Major is an administrative rank. It's been Lieutenant Colonel, Colonel, Brigadier General, Major General, Lieutenant General, and General. Now the General officers are referred to as O7, O8, O9, and O10. He has had 6 promotions."

"The General says you have a Master's Degree, Betty," said Ashley. "What did you study?"

"I have a Bachelor's Degree in Home Economics, and I graduated from Le Cordon Bleu in Paris and was awarded a Master's Degree from the Sorbonne," said Betty. "Mr. Miller paid for my European studies. He wanted me to be the best I could be."

"Well, I'll be," said Matt.

I have a meeting this morning, so I propose we continue at a dinner at the Green Room at 6:00," said the General. "We haven't had any pleasure lately, and that could be pleasant."

Everyone agreed, and group headed in its various ways. As they left, the worker said, "I wonder why they came here? I thought perhaps they were going to purchase the location."

"This is a licensed location," replied the Manager. "I'm not sure it's possible to buy out a licensed location. They probably are travelers. The younger guy and the girl next to him looked familiar. They might be from around here. Who knows.. This store is owned by Starbucks. A license is expensive and is usually held by another business, such as Target. It's kind of interesting. The Starbucks Corporation owns this location, and I think it needs an upgrade. That new Starbucks store, near here, is beating us out.

END OF CHAPTER TWO

CHAPTER 3

DINNER AT THE GREEN ROOM

"What should I wear?" asked Ashley.

"This isn't a formal event," said Matt. "I'm going to wear my teaching outfit: chinos, shirt, Oxford shoes, and sport coat. No tie, no special shirt, no anything."

"I guess I'll do the same," said Ashley. "Should I wear high heels?"

"Just wear what you wear to class," said Matt. "Here's a story a student told me. There was this family, probably his, that had a formal wedding, run by a professional wedding specialist. It was at a pricey place, music, bartender, sushi as an appetizer, the best. One part of the family consisted of a farmer, wife, and kids. They were uncomfortable and asked what to wear, and the bride said, "Wear what you wear to church." So, at the wedding, where everyone was dressed formally, in comes the farmer with work boots, Levi's, dirty work shirt, and an old weather-beaten farmer's hat. People were astonished. He was the most popular person at the event."

"Anything is okay be me," continued Matt. "This whole deal wasn't my idea. I would just as soon have a bowl of popcorn and a good movie."

"Me too," replied Ashley.

Ashley and Matt drove up, and then General was parked in the same spot at the Green Room restaurant that he owned.

"Don't say anything, smarty pants." Matt said to Ashley.

"I won't say a thing, watch me," said Ashley. "Look, he brought Anna with him. Are they still married?"

"You know they are," said Matt. "She has that incurable disease and has that ridiculous class she teaches on writing for old people – or whatever she does. He's a nice person, and she is good company for him. She is very intelligent, and I sure you remember from the writing course that we took together several years ago. Be nice, or no more popcorn and movies for you."

Matt had a funny smile on his face.

"Talk all you want," said Ashley, "I make the popcorn, get the movie CD, and turn it on. You couldn't do without me."

"You are correct there," answered Matt. "But you know what I mean."

Ashley just smiled. She had Matt wrapped around her little finger, and he loved it.

The General had the tables moved to provide an ideal place so they could talk. Ashley sat next to Matt. Anna sat next to the General, and Betty sat between the General and Ashley.

The waiter asked about drinks, and the General ordered a single malt scotch over ice, the ladies had daiquiris, and Matt ordered a bottle of S. Pelegríno's, which they didn't have. Matt took a Perrier and looked at the General, as of to say, 'They need a talking to'.

The U.S. budget situation was the topic of discussion, as it was a recurring problem. The Democrats wanted to raise the budget limit, and the Republications agreed only if the Democrats lowered spending. Then the Democrats wanted to raise taxes on the rich, and the General said, "Tax and spend; I've heard that before, but I wouldn't want to live anywhere else."

"Does anyone know what the U.S. debt is and what is the number of people in this country," asked Matt.

"You won't believe it, but I do," said Anna. "It came up yesterday in my class. The debt is 30 trillion and the U.S. population is 300 million."

"Can anyone calculate the amount per person?" Asked Matt with a smile. He was up to something and everyone noticed it.

"I can," said Betty.

Matt, Ashley, the General, and Anna turned their heads in total amazement.

"It's about $100,000 per person," said Betty. "That's 30 times 10 to the 12th, divided by 3 times 10 to the 8th, which comes out to that amount."

Matt, who thought he was the only one that could figure it out was totally out of his mind with confusion. All he said was, "How?"

"I'll tell you the story, and I hope you will believe it, because it is true," answered Betty. "When I was young in Cleveland, the best location in the nation in those days, when the boys were out playing softball in the street, we girls were inside learning how to calculate. That was my Dad's hobby. He was a math professor. He worked at Boeing in Seattle during World War II and my Mom worked on B-17 bombers assembly. They turned out 16 B-17s per day. We loved Seattle. As to the math, I went to college and they gave entry tests on math and English. They tried to talk me into being a math major but I stuck to home economics. After my training at Le Cordon Bleu, I was happy with my choice. Many people were irritated with me over my choice of my home economics over math, but I stuck to my guns and was happy with my decision. One more thing, my Dad also taught us calculus, that is my 3 sisters and myself. That was both differential and integral calculus. That really upset the people at the college. I tried to get through that college and not get any Bs, but they got me on freshman speech."

"I must say, Betty, that you are a better speaker than I, and I love to do it," said Matt. "I have many complements from students and other faculty. But, I have to say, you are much better than I ever was."

"Oh, I can explain that," said Betty. "My Dad arranged for me to attend a toastmasters course at our church, and I got better. I was so fortunate."

With the conversation of Betty, the dinner went really fast, and it – the conversation – continued until the dinner was finished.

"I just got a signal from the Maitre D," said the General, "We should wind up our dinner. This has been very good, better that I ever expected and we did not cover the things I had in mind. Can we continue at the same time tomorrow?"

Everyone nodded, 'YES', and the time was set at 6 0'clock.

"Well, I'll be," said Matt.

"You have already said that twice today," said Ashley. Two is your limit."

As usual, the rich couple that happened to be in the Green Room when the General and all the rest were also in the Green Room, had something to say about the situation. The woman said, "Things have changed. The new woman has had her share of the conversation. She talked a lot about math and calculus, and something called differential and integral. I couldn't understand all of it." Her husband was surprised. "How did you get all that information? The Woman relied, "I'm taking a correspondence course on lip reading. I do it while you are fussing over the stock market. The older gentleman and the tall young tanned person have a habit of facing in the other direction. They are trained, because I would say that people usually do not behave in that manner. " Her husband said, "Things change, I still wonder what they do. I got it. Maybe they are spying on us." The wife said, "Not funny McGee."

END OF CHAPTER THREE AND PART ONE

PART 2

The Past Comes to Life

CHAPTER 4

THE DAY BEFORE
THE BIG DINNER

The next day must have felt like the longest day ever on earth. The General, Anna, Ashley, and Betty just sat around waiting for something to happen, even though they knew nothing was going to happen until dinner time. The previous dinner was so interesting and pleasureful that their expectations were very high.

No one knew where Matt was. He disappeared. Ashley said that he was probably at home with his nose in a math book. Maybe, he was taking a nap. No one knew and no one was concerned.

They just sat around, searched TV, read a book or newspapers, and wandered around the house. The General went upstairs to his study and said he was re-affirming his reservation at the Green Room, the restaurant that he owned. He was transparent and they all knew he was up to something, and they thought it had something to do with the evenings dinner and dessert.

"I think Mr. Miller, that is the General as you refer to him, is on a health regimen," said Betty.

Ashley agreed, and Anna said he never before cared a whit about what he ate or drank.

"I can tell you why," said Ashley. "I think I am correct."

"I'm his wife, and I don't know," said Anna.

"Here is what happened," started Ashley. "In the past few months, the General was called back to active duty. When you are a general, like he is, the position entails being called back to duty when the need arises. Essentially, you are a general for life. In the case of our general, his experience was valuable. He also has a good head on his shoulders. Something happened that he had to take care of it. That kind of stuff is always secret."

Ashley continued after a sip of Diet Coke. "Matt's PhD dissertation advisor, Gregory Kacan's wife died, and it turned out to be kind of a big deal when the General was gone. I'm just talking like we are talking over a cup of coffee or in a beer joint, although I haven't ever been in a beer joint and don't exactly know what one is."

"I know what one is," said Betty. "Remember, I'm from Cleveland that had streetcars in those days that ran down the middle of the street. The streetcar stopped at a regular scheduled stopping point and the automobiles had to stop while the passengers got out and crossed to the sidewalk. These old guys would get off the streetcar, cross the traffic, and walk into a small establishment with bar stools called a beer joint. It was across the side street from a church. The old guys would order a shot and a beer before they went home."

"What's a shot?" asked Anna.

"It's a small jigger of whiskey," said Ashley with the look of how could anyone not know this.

"Either the old guy would swallow the shot and drink the beer, or put the shot in the beer and drink it," said Betty. "In the latter case, they called it a boilermaker. They said the old guys would drink a boilermaker to help them survive the wrath of their old ladies, what they called their wife in those days. The men said things like, 'My old lady always wants more money'.

The ladies looked up and there was Matt standing there with a big smile on his face.

"That's quite an intellectual conversation," said Matt. "You should turn on your cell phone and record it. However, the jest of it did sound interesting. I didn't know what a beer joint was and for sure never heard of a boilermaker."

"We had just started talking about your advisor Greg Kacan, and I made a remark since it wasn't an intellectual conversation," said Ashley. "Where were you?"

"I was in the living room reading my math book," answered Matt. "Never leave home without one."

"We had just started talking about Greg Kacan, as I said, and that is what we were involved with when you stepped up," said Ashley. "It occurred when the General was in the pentagon. I just started the conversation and since Greg Karan is your friend, Matt, why don't you take it from there?"

"It's not anything spectacular," said Matt. "The sequence of events and the context in which it occurred was kind of ironical, and maybe even interesting."

"This professor named Gregory Kacan was my advisor," continued Matt. "He married a woman named Katerina Stevens, who had a brother named Harry Steevens who has worked with us and took math courses with me. He put an extra letter 'e' in his name as a result of Harry being fed up with the fact that there was too many 'Stevens' in the world. That's who we are dealing with."

"Greg's wife died, and Harry came to tell me about it," continued Matt. "He was kind of upset, and rightly so. We decided it was most appropriate to have him visit first and then me. Harry visited Greg in their beach home and Greg was doing an admirable job of talking to himself, and also listening to himself. I'm sure we will delve into the subject when the General is with us. I sequentially visited Greg Kacan and the self-talking persisted. It looked too familiar so I contacted the General, when he was in the Pentagon as an advisor, and he put us in touch with Mark Clark, Director of National Intelligence, who put us in contact with a scientist named Hutchinson. True to form, Greg was involved with one of those secret projects that the government was running during the Cold War. Greg didn't like the looks of things and bolted. The word *bolted*, means he left without leaving a trace. Then, we, that is Ashley and I, came to the conclusion that Greg was in the process of grieving and all is okay. As I said, this is a first draft of the story."

"I think I've met Greg Kacan," said Betty.

"No kidding," said Matt. "How would you have met him?"

"There is another thing you don't know about me," added Betty. "My husband was an associate of Greg Kacan."

"What is your last name, not your maiden name but your married last name?" asked Matt.

"Roberts," answered Betty.

"Well, I'll be," said Matt.

"That's number one," said Ashley. "You have only one left, unless you want to change the quota."

"Professor Roberts was a professor for one of my math courses when I was an undergraduate," said Matt. "He was a good professor – not just good, but real good."

"He liked teaching," said Betty. "He only wrote one book and no more than one paper a year – only to get to go to a conference,"

"What was the title of the book?" asked Matt.

"Projective Geometry," answered Betty. "I typed it."

"That's the course that I took from Professor Roberts," replied Matt. "I see we are going to have an interesting dinner – maybe two more dinners. One more thing, then I'll shut up. Around college campuses, there is a saying among faculty, 'One book for your career, and one paper per year'. Most research is going nowhere, but that is known beforehand. There are a lot of ideas. A professor gets an idea, researches it, and writes a paper. Only a few of those ideas is going anywhere so the number of papers is what is important to the professor. That is a characteristic of research. That's why organizations like NASA are needed to get things done."

The General came downstairs and declared it was time for dinner.

END OF CHAPTER FOUR

CHAPTER 5

MORE INFORMATION
ABOUT BETTY

Nothing changed on the way to the Green Room. Both the General and Matt parked right in front. Of course, they weren't parking, because they were not in the parking area. No one said a word; the fun was over.

The general had done an excellent job setting up the special dinner. He had arranged a special room and the staff were dressed for a special occasion. The General, Matt, Ashley, Anna, and Betty were seated, as before. The drinks were as expected, scotch for the General, daiquiris for the ladies, and S. Pellegrino water for Matt. Everyone was in good spirits, especially the General who liked to set things up. Pleasantries were discussed and a fine Beef Bourguignon dinner was served. It was a dinner that no one, except perhaps the General, had before.

The group finished their dinner, and they just sat there, as if to say, 'What's next General? You are the person celebrating being discharged from the military'.

"Dessert anyone,' said the General. It was and wasn't a question, and it took everyone by surprise.

"Nothing for me," said Ashley followed by, "Well, if everyone want dessert, I'll give it a try."

Matt knew that Ashley had a terrific sweet tooth, and also was the best at selecting the dessert that everyone wished they had ordered.

"Okay," said the General. "I'll have apple pie with a slice of cheese."

"I've always wondered what the cheese is for," said Matt. "They always serve it in the university dining hall."

"It's to cleanse the palate," said Ashley. "They don't serve that much anymore."

"I'll have a strawberry French torte," said Matt, "with real whipped crème. How's that for class."

"I'll just have ice cream," said Betty, "My husband liked that."

"What about you, Ashley?" asked Matt.

"I'll have the same as the General," said Ashley. "I want to get on his good side."

Ashley was a bit of a joker, and loved to play around with words.

"You are already there," replied the General. "How about you, Anna?"

"I'll have chocolate cake with chocolate icing," answered Anna. "I never got enough of that when I was a kid. Yes, believe it or not, I was once a kid."

Anna liked to joke around too."

"Are you ready to order dessert?" asked the waiter.

"We'll have that special French dessert I ordered, just for this evening," replied the General.

"Well, I'll be," said Matt.

"Coffee everyone?" asked that Waiter.

"I'll have another scotch," said the General.

Coffee," said Anna and Betty together,

Ashley and Matt just looked at each other, and said, "Nothing please."

Everyone thoroughly enjoyed the Crème Brûlée, specially ordered by the General, and especially the after dessert charade by the General.

Ashley and Matt just looked at each other, as if to say, 'Older people are sure strange'.

"Tell us about your husband, Betty," said the General. "I've never asked about him before, and I would say that no one else has either."

"It will be a pleasure," replied Betty. "Up until now, it was the most enjoyable part of my life. We were married for 51 years, and I don't regret a single moment. We did everything together. We thought the same and enjoyed the same entertainment, and extra pleasantries. He never mentioned or did things he knew that I wouldn't like, and I the same."

"You lived quite long," said Matt.

"Oh, that is a story in its own right,' continued Betty. "My father was unsure about my cooking, so he gave me a healthy-eating cookbook on the evening that we were married, and I think it worked."

"How did your husband die?" asked Ashley

"He contracted an enlarged liver condition that he inherited from his father who inherited it from her father's mother, who died of it. It skipped a generation, so her father didn't get it. The day my husband died, he thanked me for a good life."

Betty started to cry, and the General asked if she would prefer to stop. Betty answered that it was best to finish once they got started.

"I should start at then beginning about my life," said Betty. "What I am was largely determined by my parents."

"That could be interesting," mentioned Matt. "Because what I am is exactly opposite, and was largely determined by my professors, and perhaps more so, by the General, who you refer to as Mr. Miller. I must say you are very polite!"

"That's true, I am polite and I think I am well educated," continued Betty. "My parents took their parental jobs seriously, but a lot of people do that but that's all. Perhaps, we were receptive to it, and it could have been the schools we went to, and then church, and the facilities provided by the city in which we lived. But when a loved one passes away, a lot of that good training seems to go away. I somehow felt like we are going to talk about those things as things progress."

"That is a good idea," said the General. "I think this is good place and an excellent way to discuss things like this. Let's do it over again in a couple of days. Let's say two days from now."

The group looked over and Anna was sound asleep.

The General and Matt planned to meet the next day for golf at the Country Club to which they both were members, along with their families and close relatives. Things had been complicated for a week or so, and they both looked forward to a good round of golf and maybe another in the afternoon. Playing golf is a lot of work, but not if you enjoy it. Then it is complete pleasure.

END OF CHAPTER FIVE

ANOTHER UNFORTUNATE SITUATION

It was 6 am and the phone rang in Ashley and Matt's bedroom. Ashley punched Matt and said, "It's your Grandfather; can you answer it? I'm occupied at the moment."

"Now I know what occupied means," said Matt. "Would you like some coffee after I tend to my usual 6 o'clock regimen of talking to my Grandfather?"

Ashley smiled, nodded and fell back to sleep.

"Good morning, Sir," said Matt. "How are you this morning?"

"Can you come over as soon as you can?" said the General. "Anna is having trouble and can't get up and get to the bathroom."

"Hold on, I'll be there as soon as I possibly can," said Matt. "I have to put on some pants and shoes. Relax. It will only be 5 minutes."

Matt jumped into his pants that were on the chair and slipped into his loafers with no socks.

"Where are my car keys?" asked Matt.

"On the table by the door," answered Ashley. "Don't get yourself killed. What happened anyway?"

"Don't know," said Matt. "Something to do with Anna."

Matt opened the garage door and hopped into his Porsche Taycan. In two minutes, he was there. The General was at the door.

Both men helped Anna into the bathroom who made a big mess. They put Anna back in bed and the General was not his usually calm person.

"I'll clean it up," said Matt. "Just get us some coffee from the Keurig."

"I don't know how to," said the General.

"I'll do it," said Ashley who had jumped into her Chevy and just came in the door. "Relax, I will take care of Anna."

Matt and the General sat in the kitchen and sipped their coffee. Ashley quieted Anna and checked her pulse.

"I'm a little worried," said Ashley. "Her heart rate is high, and I think she should go to the hospital. Are you going to take her? Use the Chevy. Here's the key. I'll finish cleaning up and then take your car. Can you give me your key fob?"

Matt and the General walked Anna to the Chevy and put her in the back seat. The university hospital was 5 minutes away and the General phoned the hospital emergency on the way.

When Ashley arrived 30 minutes later, the men were in the waiting area.

"What are you doing here?" asked Ashley. "Where is Anna?"

"They won't let us in," answered the General.

When they finally got to Anna's hospital room, she was wired up and had a smile on her face.

The physician's assistant, actually the hospital assistant who was a certified physician's assistant, told Matt, the General, and Ashley that Anna was okay.

"We'd like to keep her for an hour," said the PA, "then you can take her home. For her age, she is in good shape."

And that was it. "It might have been a close call or a wake up message to you," said the PA. "Just keep an eye on her."

"I'm really worried about her," said Matt.

Matt and the General were sitting on chairs at the kitchen table. If the General did not drink coffee, he did now.

"She has been taking that high powered medicine for her Myelofibrosis condition and it is under control," continued

Matt. 'That doctor Kabelnoff in London is a proverbial medical genius. We don't know what is happening in the rest of her body. I don't know about her eating and sleeping regimens. When she gets food, does she eat it? I'm concerned that she couldn't walk, but now she seems okay."

"I'm sorry," said the General. "She has a lady that comes to take of her. She has not said a word. But, when Anna couldn't even walk to the bathroom, it really bothered me too."

"Is the doctor treating the whole person or just the major disease that she has?" asked Matt. "Does she tell the doctor when something is wrong with her, or is she one of those people that always says that everything is okay? She has a French ancestry. Do French people avoid telling the doctor and masquerade that everything is okay with them?"

"She seemed to eat at the restaurant," said the General. "I didn't watch her because people don't like to be watched when they are eating. People could stick food in a napkin or something like that. Maybe she is starving herself. Maybe it hurts when she eats."

"I'll tell you one thing," said Matt. "Neither of the ladies finished their daiquiri drinks, as you did not finish your scotch."

"You seem to look at everything," said the General.

"I don't do it on purpose," replied Matt. "I think it is in my genes. It's that way when I walk into a room, I see and remember every detail. I guess that was why I was such a good math student. I remembered every squiggly symbol, as Ashley puts it, that the math prof put on the board. I think we should wait and see how things turn out. I do not live here, but you do. So I would say the ball is in your court."

"She still has that studio and that writing class," added the General. "It's infrequent, but she has stayed there overnight. Her class runs from 6:30 to 9:00 so I suppose that she is sometimes tired at the end of the day."

"Ashley and I will help all we can," added Matt. "We don't live here and are both not medically proficient. We are going home now. Let us know if something happens and we will be here in 5 minutes. I'll sleep with my clothes on."

Matt and Ashley had two cars at the General's home, so they didn't have a chance to discuss the situation. Both were tired and had work of their own.

The General postponed the next dinner until things settle down.

Two weeks later, Anna's systems were totally inoperable. All of her systems: blood pressure, heart, liver, and kidneys had broken down. The General called 911 and an ambulance took her to the same university hospital. She passed away in two hours.

The General was totally distraught. Matt had never seen him in such a miserable condition. He just sat in the living room. He wouldn't or couldn't talk, eat, or sleep. Matt and Ashley were at their wits end.

In a few days, the General appeared to be back to his usual self. He rescheduled the dinner at the Green Room. On the surface he was back to his usual self. Not quite. He parked his car in the parking lot.

Matt and the General scheduled a round of golf at the country club. After the 9th hole, the General started discussing Anna's death. Matt was surprised at his candor.

"Matt, I haven't done a single thing since Doodles died. We had private names for each other. Every time I do something, I say something to her. But she is not there, of course. I came home and I said, 'Doodles, I'm home.' When I go to the bathroom, I say, 'Doodles, I'll be right back." I wake up and look over at her in our bed. She isn't there. Sometimes, I look up from the table or my chair, and I see her for a flash second. I spend all day wishing she were here. Here's what I eat. Bran cereal for breakfast, nothing more. A container of yogurt for lunch. A sandwich and chips for dinner. I don't drink anything but water. After I get up, I make the bed, before I even go to the bathroom. Every time that I pass the laundry room, I run a load of clothes. This round of golf is my first step outside of the house. All I think of is the things we did together. I suppose I will get over it. You are the first person I've told."

"For dinner, is it all right if I invite Greg Kacan and Harry Steevens?" asked Matt. "Greg's wife is Harry's sister. They were close."

"Sure Matt," said the General. "That may help. Matt, you're the best."

END OF CHAPTER SIX AND PART TWO

PART 3

The Past Comes to Life

CHAPTER 7

WHAT IS REALLY HAPPENING WITH GREG

A cell phone rang in Matt and Ashley's home, and Ashley picked it up.

"May I speak with Matt, please?" asked Harry Steevens.

"Sure, I'll get him," said Ashley.

Matt was shuffling through some papers and pressed the green phone button on his cell phone.

"Hi Harry," said Matt. "What's up?"

"How did you know it is me?" asked Harry.

"You're in my directory," said Matt.

"I forgot," said Harry. "Can I come over for a few minutes?"

"Sure," said Matt. "Come around the back. We were just about to have some tea - so to speak."

Harry arrived in about a minute. He had called in his car nearby.

"Like some iced tea, Harry?" asked Ashley.

"No thanks," said Harry as he sat down. "I'll be but a few minutes."

"You look distressed," said Matt.

"I am," said Harry. "I visited Greg just 10 minutes ago, and he is worse than ever. He thinks he is going to visit with Kat."

"Who's Kat?" asked Ashley.

"That is Harry's sister," said Matt.

"Sorry," said Ashley. "I wasn't thinking."

"How is he going to do that?" asked Matt.

"This voice that he talks to is going to do it," said Harry. "He's got Greg all excited about it. I was listening when Greg didn't know it. This voice has convinced Greg that when a person dies, their soul or brain or something goes into a very small orb and they are like some extremely small particle, like a neutrino, and there a trillion of them in the universe and people can't see them, like we can't see neutrinos. He convinced Greg that Kat is in one of those things that they call an *ope*. Some opes can talk and some can't, and there are conditions that apply. Like if no one visits them when the body is interred, then they can't talk. But if you visit the site of interment, then they can talk. They even have made up that the ones can live in two Spaces: a Hope Space and a Unicorn Space. Ops in the Hope

Space can talk, and the Unicorn space can't. So Greg asked how they could find Kay's op, and the voice said the only an ope that can talk can find other ones that can talk. Actually, it is clever. An ope from a Hope Space is the only kind of ope that can go into the Hope Space to find an ope that can talk. Greg would be led to Kay's ope by the voice ope. I'm in law enforcement as a profession, and would you like to hear what I think?"

"I would like to hear what you think, but I have already figured it out," said Matt.

"You're on candid camera," said Harry.

"It's a con game," said Matt.

"That's what I think," said Harry.

"Did you record this Ashley?" asked Matt.

"Sure did Matt," said Ashley. "I can read your mind. Would you also like to hear the second part?"

"Now I can read both of your minds," said Harry. "You would like to go to the Green Room to make a plan."

"Well, I'll be," said Matt.

"Are you free, Harry," continued Matt.

"Now I am," said Harry.

END OF CHAPTER SEVEN

CHAPTER 8

WORKING UP A PLAN

The three warriors pulled up to the Green Room and parked right in front. The sign said NO PARKING.

"It says no parking," said Ashley. "You're going to get a ticket."

"That would be the first time in history," said Harry. "A cop giving a cop a parking ticket."

The Maitre'D recognized Matt and Ashley, gave them a good table where they couldn't be seen. All three pulled out a notebook.

"I recommend a prime fillet, a loaded baked potato, green salad, and a Diet Coke," said Matt. "I'm paying. Let's get going."

"Where do you think we should start, Ashley?" asked Matt.

"I think that we should establish that Greg's motivation and behavior is reasonable when a spouse of several years passes away," said Ashley. "We have two examples: Betty and the General. We have to talk to them about it."

"We should establish and verify that what the government was trying to do was indeed cancelled before Greg was involved, and it was a reasonable thing to do during a Cold War," said Matt. "We can't let it be thought that it was a purely normal thing to do."

"We should make sure that what the voice is doing is illegal," said Harry,

"What do we do once we get all of this information?" said Ashley.

"How do we find who is doing the con?" said Harry. "It has to be done electronically. Who and how?"

"Assuming Greg has to pay some money, which is the con, how would that take place?" said Matt.

"I wonder if we could get Greg to help us in that regard," said Ashley.

"That wouldn't work," said Matt. "The con artists would easily find out and close down the operation."

"I think we should describe the situation and turn it over to the government," said Harry. "They have experience doing things like this."

The food arrived.

"Let's eat and then decide what to do tomorrow," said Matt.

"Dessert anyone?" asked Matt, "I'm going to try apple pie with a slice of cheese to test my palate."

"Sound good," said Harry,

"Why of course," said Ashley.

"I think we should get the General on board and visit that Dr. Hutchinson in the Pentagon to see if there is any additional information on the Unicorn Project that he didn't tell us in the first meeting, and I will contact Kimberly Scott in Washington to see if there is any information on the capability to have a person beam information to another person," said Matt.

"We've done enough for one day," said Ashley.

END OF CHAPTER EIGHT

CHAPTER 9

THE GENERAL GETS INVOLVED

Matt contacted the General who was enthused about being involved in the latest development in then Unicorn Project. For him, it was a break in the action of grieving over Anna and all of the useless activity surrounding a person that was grieving.

The General called Mark Clark, the Director of National Intelligence, who was sympathetic to the General's request and scheduled a meeting the next morning with Dr. Hutchinson in his office in the Pentagon. He ordered a 7:30 pickup at the New Jersey local airport in a presidential C40 for Ashley, Matt, the General, Harry Steevens, and Betty Roberts. He reserved a slot for Greg Kacan, pending it turned out to be appropriate. He reminded the General that a defensive subject may cast a defensive nature to their meeting. Then General decided against it. The General wanted to hear from Kimberly Scott on the communications side of the picture. The General reminded Clark that they needed ID cards and the Director said that he knew it. Their last visit had caused him a bit of trouble, as they were fooling no one with their age-old cards.

Matt called Kimberly. "Hi Kimberly, how is my favorite analyst?"

"Hi Matt, it's good to hear from you. I hope you have a hard problem for me," said Kimberly. "You're my best customer."

"Do you have a thing with her," said Harry,

"I heard that Harry Steevens; I picked you up in three words, now that we have people's voices recorded"

"Well', I'll be," said Matt.

"That's kind of related to our problem," said Matt. "There is this person who is grieving and thinks he is verbally corresponding with a voice from a person that is not alive…

"I'm sorry to interrupt you, Matt, but we know all about that story," said Kimberly. "Part of Hutchinson's contract is that has to report all activity to us, but we do not have to report to him. We have this genius working here, and he had it figured out before he went home that evening. I do not even know who he is and where he works. We have this device the size of a cell phone, actually it is a cell phone, that identifies non-directed speech and gives a location of the sender and the responding person."

"That's how you picked out who Harry was a minute ago?" said Matt.

"That's part of it," said Kimberly. "Hutchinson doesn't know about it but he will be cleared before you get there tomorrow, so will you and Harry be cleared. Remember, no talking about it, except with Hutchinson. It also goes for your guests on the C40 flight at 7:30 tomorrow. We will pick their voices up during the flight. I'll have the device to your home in three hours with documentation. If you are looking for this person, who is doing the dirty work, and I believe you are, I would venture to say that he is a goner."

"Thanks Kimberly, you are the best," said Matt.

"You are too, Matt," but you're a bigger best.

"I'll get a limo, so let's meet here at 7:00 am tomorrow," said the General. "Bring your state ID card and your passport. Wear business attire. Don't be late. My cook will have something to eat. Better come at 6:30 if you want to eat."

"Sounds good," said Ashley. "He is back to normal – a little at least."

"This will be good for Betty and Harry," said the Matt on the way home with Ashley, "Betty and the General have the same situation. This could be interesting,"

Matt's cell phone signaled a call. "A round of golf," said the General. Ashley nodded 'yes' and Matt agreed. "He really is getting back to normal," said Ashley. Matt just gave a sigh of relief.

END OF CHAPTER NINE AND PART THREE

PART 4

Analyzing the Situation

BACK TO THE PENTAGON

At Matt's request, the General's cook prepared a small breakfast of yogurt, a scone, and coffee. No one was overjoyed, pleased, or anything else. They were just plain nervous. A C40 presidential jet was one thing, but visiting the Pentagon was another.

It seemed like everyone was annoyed, except perhaps Harry. The General was annoyed because he would be an ordinary citizen, and not a big shot General. Betty was annoyed because she did not know what she was supposed to do. Matt was annoyed because he had to pretend he knew what was going on when he did know what was going on. Ashley was annoyed because she did not like Hutchinson and she had to put up with him. Harry wasn't annoyed at all and spent his time snitching other people's scones.

Ashley asked Harry if he was wearing his ankle beretta and he pulled up his pant leg. Nothing. Then he patted his hip and said, "I have my real gun right here."

"You had better leave that thing here or your worst dreams will come true," said the General. "Let me tell you a little story, and it's really true. After my buddy, Buzz, and I were promoted to Captain and ordered to report to the Pentagon, we got stopped because our bars were on side ways. This Marine confronted Buzz, being a tough guy, threw the Marine on is tail. Can you imagine it. It was war time. Another Officer came along and told Buzz that the Marine was nervous because he thought Buzz and I were spies. He told the Marine that if he didn't watch he would be headed to the front line. How would we know how to put on our bars, we were fighter pilots. Okay, it's a dumb story."

On the flight to Washington, Matt told about the two earlier scenarios that Harry had with Greg Kacan, he and passed out commented copies, as follows:

"He did notalk to me very much, except to exchange pleasantries," said Harry. "The problem was that Greg got into a conversation with someone else and there was no one for me to converse with. He talked at great length with someone, but I am sorry to say, I could not determine who he was talking to. It wasn't like a dream, but rather a give and take conversation in which the other person was running the conversation. It was like the other person was telling Greg something. It was a weird conversation. There was no other person and only Greg was talking. When you visit with him, record the conversation secretly on your cell phone. Perhaps you can make something out of it. I don't feel like visiting Greg again."

> The conversation centered around the problem of how Greg could talk to Kat. Kat had died and was cremated. Assuming that an afterlife exists, they had to find out where she was and then turn her on, so to speak, so they could converse.

That information Matt could deduce from the conversation. Only Greg seemed to be talking.

They didn't know if Kat had the capability for speech and if so, was it turned on or how to turn it on?

The voice that Greg was talking to was under the opinion that Kat was an *ope*, and would not be able to speak to Greg unless the voice – they started to call her an *ope* – turned the *ope* on. When she died, her capability for conversation was not available or turned on and the voice thought he could do it. This information Matt was able to deduce from the conversation.

Next, they didn't know where the Kat *ope* was. Assuming she was a particle in the form of an org of some sort, maybe the wind or the gravitational force of another planet carried her away.

Assuming that Kat's *ope* was nearby where she was interred, the question was how to get the voice *ope* to where the Kat *ope* was.

The voice *ope* could not propel itself but was somehow attracted to Greg. They discussed that for a good 15 minutes. They figured out a method by which the voice *ope* could trail Greg to the place of interment.

Matt was amazed. The level of creativity was huge.

The big question turned out to be how would they recognize the Kat *ope* when they found her.

Matt noticed that it was not a normal human-to-human conversation. Many of the remark were entangled as if they were coming from the same person. It was like Greg's brain was talking and then told him what to hear. I short, Greg was answering his own speech. It seemed as though Greg's brain was telling itself and Greg didn't know it. .

Then in a flash, Matt had it. Greg's brain was commanding him. It was like when a soldier was in combat, there was someone giving orders, but that person was itself.

Matt turned off his recorder, he had enough. This was a job for the intelligence community.

"This is what we are going to talk with Dr. Hutchinson about," said Matt. "They did have a project named the *Unicorn Project* that did have an objective of having a soldier be in a position to command himself in certain circumstances that we didn't cover. The project was aborted because Greg Kacan left the project without prior notice. He bolted, as they say. As Dr. Hutchinson said, they had not gotten far enough in the project to do anything. I believed him and still do. We are here to confirm that the previous assessment was correct. That's it. I personally think everything that we learned so far is the truth."

"Maybe this person, Greg Kacan, has mental difficulties," said Betty. "When my husband died, I was completely aware that I could not communicate with him. Nevertheless, there were countless instances that my response to a situation, like waking up in the morning, when it was rote behavior that I said 'morning' or I closed the bathroom door tightly or I said 'watch out for the step'. There was no explicit thinking involved. But when there was thinking involved, I behaved normally."

"What about you General, even though not enough time has taken place for you to get a complete assessment?" asked Matt.

"I just sit there like a stump," said the General. "But I do think that If I had a picture of Anna sitting there I would talk to her."

"What about when a spouse goes to the place the deceased is interred, the visitor is thought to tell the decease person what is going on and so forth?" asked Ashley. "Does this behavior ever go away?"

"I guarantee to you that it does in fact go away, but in some cases it takes a long time and in others, it is almost immediate," said Betty. "If you have been married for a long time, I think there is a lot to talk about. I have talked to some people in this regard."

"The limo is here everybody," said the General. "Let's get cracking."

The presidential C40 was waiting on the runway. The airport was otherwise closed for 30 minutes. The normal passengers complained like the dickens. All the airport employees could say was that the airport was closed for government business. The pilots will make up the time.

The presidential pilots were cheerful, which was unusual.

"Which one of you is the General?" asked the First Officer with a smile on his face.

He knew full well that the older gentleman had to be the general, but was working on the General's ego.

"I am," said Betty. "You guys better fly good or you are in big trouble."

The Captain and the First Officer laughed as did everyone else besides the real General.

As the plane taxied for takeoff, the General said, "Hit the afterburner."

"It doesn't have one," said the Captain. "Oh, here it is. Hang on."

The people waiting in the lobby got the show of their lives, as the airplane took off at a 45 degree angle.

The Captain said, "This hasn't happened since 9/11when President Bush took off in Florida in Air Force One."

The C40 landed at Dulles Airport to a waiting Marine One helicopter. In a few minutes, they were in Dr. Hutchinson's spacious office.

END OF CHAPTER TEN

CHAPTER 11

COMPARING PERSONAL EXPERIENCES

The General was seated next to Matt and whispered something. Matt looked at his notes and stood up.

"I feel like sleeping, just as everyone else, but perhaps this is a good time to discuss personal experiences when grieving, before we go into Dr. Hutchinson's office," said Matt. "He probably like the rest of them think they know everything, I'll admit that he might know a lot about deaths and grieving, but I feel quite certain that he doesn't know everything. So, let's talk about the subject. We have three people that can help us: Harry, Betty, and the General. Harry's information is remote, but he is an extremely intelligent guy and can give us another perspective. Let's let him talk first. No comments, please, just listening."

"Katarina Kacan, Greg's wife who died, was my sister and before they married, she and I were very close. We helped each other, sided for each other against our parents, and did things together. We even jumped out of an airplane together, as well as doing sports, such as water skiing and snowboarding. When she was happy or sad, she confided with me and I, the same. I was Greg's best man at their wedding. I admit that I didn't exactly miss her, because we did not live together. When I entered the house, I was not used to saying something like, 'Hi Kat, I'm back'. When we were together, such as Christmas or Easter, we were cordial. I would do anything for her, and she the same. When I think about her, I miss her, but she is not a part of my life and I wasn't part of hers. I admit that when I think about her, I get very sad. To sum up, I still care about her."

"How about you Betty," said Matt. "Do you have anything that might be enlightening?"

"My name is Betty Roberts, and I was married to George Roberts who died from a liver disease. We were married more than 50 years and were exceedingly close. I knew how he would feel about things, and he felt the same way. Our earlier years were very similar, with one major difference. Neither of our families had very much money, but we were secure and our younger years were pleasant. Nothing bad ever happened, but then nothing very good happened. Both of our families were church-oriented, and we were as well. My father was a professor and in those days, professors didn't make much money. My husband's father changed jobs and eventually became quite successful. Our home lives were very similar. Nothing bad happened to pull us together but kids were to be seen and not heard. In those days, folks visited each other on Sunday afternoon, after church and a nice Sunday dinner. Here are a couple of stories. Remember, we lived in Cleveland and at the time, it was a great metropolis. Baseball was big and boys and men participated in sand lot organizations running from class F to class A. Class A was like the top of the minor league. When the great Bob Feller came up from the farm, he went immediately to class A. My father played class A. He had a friend who visited from time to time on a Sunday afternoon. He was a good player but his father said 'To the major league or work, no minor league'. He chewed tobacco, and when he visited he needed a can to spit into. My brother who was quite a character, systematically went from a large tomato can to a tiny tomato can and the friend never missed. My mother was always afraid for her new carpet. Here is a story from my husband's side. His mother had a friend she worked with who came over with her husband on a Sunday and said they were running out of money and needed some to tide them over. So his mother and father lent them $100 that was a lot in those days. They never saw the people again. When my husband or one of his brothers or sisters asked about, his father would calmly say, 'They will pay it back when they are ready". That was our lives, we needed someone to be nice to us. We both needed that and we got it through our marriage. We were very happy and did almost everything together. I was very very lonesome, sad, and never knew what to do with myself. In short, I needed something. I had a degree in home economics and Mr. Miller hired me as his housekeeper. He subsequently paid for my education at Le Corton Bleu in Paris and a Master's degree from the Sorbonne. Now I help him run his house. He is a very busy man, and works with Matt and Ashley, who are his best friends and business partners. I'm sorry that I talked so much, but am very fortunate to be with you folks."

Everyone clapped. Betty was a good speaker.

"It's your turn General," said Matt. "You have a tough act to follow."

"I do indeed," said the General. "I am very fortunate to have Matt and Ashley to work with and Matt to play golf with. Anna was a late addition. My first wife died a few years ago and I was a little distraught at first. She was a good woman, wife, and mother. I missed her, but bounced right back. Anna was something out of this world. She came to me as s distinguished professor and noted writer. She had a mind of her own and could figure out anything, and certainly let me know when she had an opinion. She was more than real life and I thought that I could not do without her. I miss her every second of the day and night, and the first I thing I think or say is, 'What would Anna say'. I short, I am not sure that I can do without her. That's about it."

"Well done General," said Matt. "It has only been a few days since Anna passed away."

The First Officer interrupted, "We are approaching Dulles. Please make sure your seatbelt is fastened."

END OF CHAPTER ELEVEN

CHAPTER 12

MEETING WITH DR. HUTCHINSON

Ashley, Betty, Harry, Matt, and the General were escorted into Dr. Hutchinson's spacious and were introduced to his staff of noted scientists.

"I know why you are here from your last visit and nothing in that domain has changed, said Hutchinson. "One thing that I didn't tell you is that my wife died 5 years ago and I think I have some familiarity with what some of you are going through. I think that Betty, Harry, and the General have some recent experience. I'm a psychologist and I have experience looking at people. It is somewhat like the general officer who after 30 years of experience can tell what a person is thinking and what they are going to say. Harry's experience is remote, the General's is very recent, and Betty's is a few years ago. Betty, you look like my sister, and she is very beautiful."

Betty blushed and the General whispered to Matt, "I knew it. I could tell by the way he looked at her."

"I think that Gregory Kacan was a problem right from the start," continued Hutch. "Every step we took, he wanted to know why. He absolutely could not settle down. Things got worse went he got to the statement-response exercise. The psychologist gives a scenario and the subject had to decide what to do. The scenarios and actions were known beforehand. He continually asked why he had to do that. Another problem was that he wanted to write everything down, and we wanted the activities to be dynamic. Bing. Bing. Bing. He really didn't like that. I think he hated it. He did not at all mind when we told him what to do, but he did not like to decide what to do on his own. Then he left unexpectedly. He bolted, as Matt said, which means, I guess, that he left no reason or information where was going."

"He still talked to that voice for long periods of time," said Harry. "I am in the room and it is like I am not even there. In my last visit, they were figuring out how to locate his wife's ope and how to get to where it is. He seems to be content she was in a little org about the size of a neutrino, and that there were trillions of them floating around in the universe. No one ever went away, they just couldn't be found. Both the voice and Greg were very intelligent."

Then, right out of the blue, Matt gave it away or thought he did. He mentioned the possibility of some electric device that could fool Greg and somehow get some money out of him. A con job, as they call it. That lit up Hutch like a Christmas tree. He stood up and could hardly contain himself. He stood up. Sat down. Stood up again. And then muttered," Matt you got it. You're a genius."

"There is a guy downstairs in this building that has a machine that does that,' said Hutch. "We got a patent for him. One of those secret patients they use for government secrets. Nobody is supposed to know about it. Kimberly should not have mentioned it. She misunderstood the connection."

"Do you think it is a con job?" asked the General.

"Heavens no," said Hutch. "It is just some guy that just likes to play around with his electronics and about every 6 months, he comes up with some genius idea. Those ideas often end up in fighter plane or submarines. "Here's an example. Some person at an airplane company was playing around with a toy airplane. You know how in a fighter the thrust from the engine goes straight out and it's hard to turn. So he or she made it possible to move the thrust around to more easily move the fighter plane up or down or side to side. It's called *thrust vectoring* and they have it in the F22 Raptor airplane. That's how some of those things get invented."

"Well, I'll be," said Matt.

"How did it get from here to New Jersey and how it works is the question," said Harry.

"'it seems like a radio to me but without the receiver," said. Betty. "They could send the voice to a specific latitude and longitude."

"That could be it," said Matt.

"Why not go to the government and let them figure it out," said Ashley. "The General is buddies with the Director of Intelligence, Mark Clark, and he won't mind doing it. Maybe."

"It looks like you've got it," said Hutch. I can provide your group with a meal ticket and schedule a flight back in a plane with an afterburner. We were informed of the afterburner incident regarding General Miller on your flight from New Jersey. It is our pleasure."

END OF CHAPTER TWELVE AND PART FOUR

PART 5

Analyzing the Situation

CHAPTER 13

CONTACTING THE DIRECTOR OF INTELLIGENCE

They were no more then 5 minutes into the flight when the General started in. He was not pleased, irritated, nervous, and anything more you can think of. In short, he wasn't happy and he wanted everyone to know that. The others were happy to get out of the Pentagon. Everything there was overdone. Too busy. Too complicated. Too cumbersome. Too unpleasant. Too military. And too unnecessary.

What's the first step?" asked Matt.

No one answered.

"I'd rather be on the New Jersey Turnpike chasing speeders," said Harry.

"I'd rather be dealing with the cook and the fat cleaning lady," said Betty.

"I got it," said Matt. "It is up to me. Well, here goes. We have to contact Mark Clark, Director of Intelligence, to find out exactly and precisely what is going on with this electronic device that produces the sound to which our friend Greg Kacan is responding. Is it a con game in which someone will ask for money in the future. Is it a couple of kids screwing around. Why are things so screwed up with Kimberly that she thought it was something new. What's with this Greg Kacan, my former friend, that is responding to the voice in the manner in which he is. What about this basement genius? Is the problem the device? Are they just testing it in a real life situation. Should these jokers that are producing the device be resting in prison somewhere. Perhaps they should be given a medal for achievement. Why when Greg Kacan went to Switzerland to give his talk on Reverse Mathematics was he so *successful*? They loved him asked him to come to Switzerland. Some professor said to me, 'He is so Swiss, we need him here.' And my last question is, 'Are there some guys somewhere sitting there laughing us?' "

"It looks like the ball is in your court General, said Ashley. "Perhaps, you should go to the back of this aircraft, and call Mark Clark, Director of Intelligence, on your satellite phone."

The General came back in twenty minutes. His face was a little red. He plopped down on the seat. He did not say a word. Not a single word from a person that often had the last word on practically every problem or situations.

"Did you this guy Clark?" asked Harry, who was not the least bit threatened or impressed by all of the military stuff. "What did he have to say General?"

Matt smiled and so did Ashley. They could read each other's minds. There was a solution to the problem and the General should have solved it. More was expected from a U.S. General Officer. Mark Clark, Director of Intelligence and former Chief of Staff, told that to General Miller. Moreover, why did Matt Miller and Ashley Miller not assist the General in that regard?

So, the General started out. He stood up, and cleared his throat 3 times.

"I did get in touch with him," said General. "He was not happy with our performance in this regard. He said that we should have been ready to address the problem and solve it without his assistance. However, he said that he runs a tight ship and would have a complete report on the problem by the time we landed in New Jersey. He has the power of the whole U.S. Government at his disposal and the problem was readily solved. He did tell me an important fact that we hadn't thought of probably because we didn't have the resources to determine that fact. The conversation was only one way. It was like non-directive counseling. The voice was providing and Greg Kacan was hearing general statements that were prepared beforehand. Greg Kacan responses were not a factor in the 'replies' that were sent to him. Kacan just thought that they were some sort of interactions. Remember, he said, nothing had taken place so far. It was only useless babbling. The electric device that was involved is not a part of the secret methodology of the United States. The transmission will be stopped immediately and the persons involved would be complemented for producing a useful item for the country."

The General got up and got himself a cup of coffee.

END OF CHAPTER THIRTEEN

THE SOLUTION IN A NUTSHELL

The group led by the General did not have the report when they landed in New Jersey. It had been printed and was on the printer in the General's study. Matt had said that was where it would be. Why? Because the Director asked someone to pass it on to General Miller in New Jersey, and that was the only way that person knew to transmit it.

The memo was addressed to the General, apologizing for a list rather than a written document, because it is a low priority issue. The title was: **Memo from the Director of National Intelligence to the Team Led by General Les Miller, O10. Title: Disposition of the Gregory Kacan Incident Related to the Unicorn Project Directed by General Hutchinson, MD, PhD, PsychD.** Date: 7 June 2023.

- This is not a problem of National Secretary.
- This situation is not classed as 'U.S. Secret'.
- The problem involves a grieving spouse communicating with a deceased spouse.
- Communicating with a deceased spouse is often regarded as part of the grieving process.

- The scenario involves the location of the spouse in an orb likely regarded as the size of a neutrino that exists in space.
- The existence of life after death in the stated form has not been verified by existing research.
- The subject is a U.S. citizen.
- The citizen communicates with an org who is stated to prove the necessary capability.
- The location of the spouse's orb, referred to as as *ope* is not known and is an open item.
- A conversation between the subject and the voice orb has been recorded.
- The communicating signal is emanated in free space.
- Its location is determined by latitude and longitude.
- The location of the communicating element is not known to change in a conversation.
- The proclamation from the communicating device and the subject is not related,
- The process appears to be related to non-directive counseling in Psychology.
- The device generating the voice is standard radio technology.
- There is a broadcast device but no receiver.
- The process may employ Artificial Intelligence (AI).
- There is no verification of the AI process.
- The broadcasting voice and the generated voice are not related, except by accident.
- The persons using the advanced technology are U.S. citizens employed by the U.S. Government.
- It is recommended that the test sequence for the voice system employ another subject.

- It is recommended that the grieving spouse seek other activity.
- The grieving spouse was employed as a professor of mathematics and that possibility is recommended.

This memo is not part of the governmental record and should be destroyed after 30 days.

Case closed.

Mark Clark
Direct of Intelligence and former O10 officer.
Signed
Mark Carter DI
7 June 2023

END OF CHAPTER FOURTEEN

CHAPTER 15

WHAT HAPPENED
TO THE PEOPLE

It's always interesting in a story to know what happened to the people.

Matt and Ashley are still teaching. Matt still covers one grad course, one undergrad course, and advises one graduate student during each semester. He was subsequently promoted to Department Chairperson, Dean of the College of Arts and Sciences, and finally Provost, usually regarded as the Vice President of Academic Affairs. Ashley is now the Dean of Academic Activities after service as Department Chairperson of the Drama Department. Her main hobby and extracurricular activity is quilting.

Professor Gregory Kacan teaches Reverse Mathematics in the Mathematics Department at the university in Switzerland. Harp Thomas, Matt's college buddy, and his wife moved to a big home on the East Coast of the Lake of Zürich. Harp is Department Chairman in Mathematics. He with his wife Kimberly Jensen now have three children. Gregory Kacan has taken Harp's apartment across the street from the Storchen Hotel on the Rennweg in Zürich, Switzerland.

Betty has married Dr. Hutchinson who moved to New Jersey to be with Betty. Hutch took a liking to her at their first meeting, since she looked like his sister who is very pretty. Hutch has a chair in the Psychology Department and directs advanced research. They were married in an elaborate church wedding in Cranbury, New Jersey being driven there is a classic Rolls Royce automobile. The joyous couple honeymooned in Klosters, Switzerland.

The General, of course, deserves a chapter of his own.

END OF CHAPTER FIFTEEN AND PART FIVE

PART 6

Back to Normal

CHAPTER 16

TO LONDON

After sitting around for several weeks, the General called at the usual time of 6 am and asked about a round of golf at 10 am. Ashley was annoyed at being awakened for such as a routine round of golf. Matt, on the other hand, was very pleased. Perhaps the General was getting back to normal. Matt brought Ashley a fresh cup from their Keurig and offered her a breakfast at Starbucks. Ashley was kind of pleased but thought there were more 6 o'clocks to come.

The General was there and he had parked in the parking lot in the rear of the building. Ashley, always the one to figure things out, was more than curious.

"He's up to something," said Ashley as she and Matt got out of the car.

"You may be correct," replied Matt.

They got a table near the window out of the vision of nosey people with nothing to do. Now that people are supposedly working at home, they was plenty of time for loafing at Starbucks.

Matt had his usual yogurt, scone, and a venti coffee. Ashley and the General had a breakfast sandwich, potatoes, and only a smaller grande coffee. For some strange reason, everyone was in celebratory mood.

"There is something going on," said Matt. "Has the Government eliminated the income tax, or something?"

"Not that I know of," replied the General, "Except that I am thinking about a trip to London to see what going on."

"You already know that Mr. General; absolutely positively nothing," said Ashley, with that look on her face like she had said something humorous.

"Not when I'm there," said the General. "I'm going to give Buzz a jingle when I get back home."

"Why don't you call him now," remarked Matt. "You have your satellite phone on your wrist that you probably haven't used since you talked to Mark Clark."

"Well, with your kind implicit permission," returned the General, "I'll do that right now."

The General dialed Buzz, who was his wing man when flying F-51 fighters in World War II. Buzz, better known a Sir Charles Bunday, was the General's lifelong friend.

"Bunday, here," said Buzz.

"Buzz, this is Les, you sound a little strange," said the General. "Did you win the lottery or something?"

"Quite the opposite," said Buzz. "Eleanor died last week, and I tell you Les, I have never been this distraught for something, but I don't know what to do."

"Sorry to hear that, Buzz, she was a big part of your life, and you always said that she was a big part of your amazing success," said General. "That's the way I felt three weeks ago when Anna passed. It's not the same, I know, but I can sympathize with you."

"Can you come over?" asked Buzz. "I need someone to have a few pints with."

"You know me better than I do," said the General. "Just get me a landing slot at London City Airport and enough time to get a pilot and fuel up, and I'll be there."

"How about tomorrow afternoon," replied Buzz. "The weather is nice here."

"I don't think I can get a pilot that soon…," the General started to say but got interrupted.

"Matt," said Buzz. "He can fly a G650. Why, by the way, did you buy a G650 rather than a B747? A trick to distract the General about the pilot situation."

"A G650 cost about $73 million and a B747 is about $400 million," said the General. "That's why."

Ashley nodded her head with approval. Everyone knew she ran the show.

"Okay," said Matt. "If you will be the First Officer."

Matt set the height at 60,000 feet and the speed at 600 and set the auto pilot. They flew a nonstop great circle route. Ashley had the whole passenger area to herself. She brought her circular quilting frame, sandwiches, and a full load of Diet Coke. The pilots, being Matt and the General, brought their Rubik's cubes. Life is good.

Upon arrival, Buzz picked them up in his large Jaguar SUV and they were off to his home in the country. The housekeeper, paid for by the royalty, was sitting in the kitchen with a cup of tea and a biscuit. The house was like a ghost town,

"I see what you said and now I know why," said the General. "Ashley, Matt, and I can help. We understand completely."

"I know about death and grieving, Les," said Buzz. "I received a lot of literature from the hospice. This is different. I can tell you why. In my household, everything was calm. My father worked through the war, there was no conflict, we went on a vacation every year, my father never changed his job from the start of his first position at 18 years until he retired at 65. My mother and Father had their clubs and the church. They were fully occupied. I was in the way. I came along and spoiled their wonderful life. No one was ever nice to me. I asked my mother a million times, 'Why was I born if everything I do is wrong. I've never had trouble, did well in school to make you proud of me, and am a pleasant person – as my friends say. Once, years and years ago, after our first child was born, my parents visited and my Mother followed Eleanor around incessantly. Eleanor said to her, why don't you spend some time with your son – that's me – and my Mother said, 'I'd rather talk to you. That happened several times. I remember them. No one ever said that they loved me. Not once. Until Eleanore can along and she was nice to me. That is all I wanted in the whole world. I just can't put Eleanor aside. All I wanted was to have someone be nice to me. What people do not realize is that there is a personal side to grieving and that is rarely if ever taken into consideration."

"I think we should go for a walk," said Ashley to Matt, and they did.

"I wonder if that is the reason the General is so nice to people, helping them, and trying to help them be better people in their own way," said Matt.

"I think you are right," replied Ashley. "The only solution I can think of is to visit the deceased's place of interment until things get better."

END OF CHAPTER SIXTEEN

CHAPTER 17

THE ROYAL WEDDING

The General's visit with Buzz lasted only three days. Ashley and Matt had their classes and if the General stayed, Matt would need a First Officer for the long flight home. In those three days, the General made good use of his time. Ashley, Matt, and Buzz remembered the General's meeting of the pretty woman on the muddy road between British air bases during the war. They pulled her back on the road and gave her chocolate and nylon stockings. It was here where the General said, "You look like my sister, she was very pretty." Both he and the Queen remembered that dreadful day. Subsequently, the Queen had their first date, and many more after her retirement as queen and renamed by the Royal Lexicographer as Katherine Penelope Radcliffe. Subsequently, her husband the consort King passed away and she was alone.

It is not known what the retired Queen and the General discussed about death and grieving. All we know is that on July 15, 2023 the two were married in a Royal ceremony. Their future residence is not known at this time. Amen.

END OF CHAPTER SEVENTEEN PART SIX AND THE BOOK

Thanks for Reading the Book
The Author

ABOUT THE AUTHOR

Harry Katzan, Jr. is a professor who has written several books and many papers on computers and service, in addition to some novels. He has been an advisor to the executive board of a major bank and a general consultant on various disciplines. He and his wife have lived in Switzerland where he was a banking consultant and a visiting professor. He is an avid runner and has completed 94 marathons including Boston 13 times and New York 14 times. He holds bachelors, masters, and doctorate degrees.

BOOKS BY HARRY KATZAN, JR.

Computers and Information Systems

Advanced Programming
APL Programming and Computer Techniques
APL Users Guide
Computer Organization and the System/370
A PL/I Approach to Programming Languages
Introduction to Programming Languages
Operating Systems
Information Technology
Computer Data Security
Introduction to Computer Science
Computer Systems Organization and Programming
Computer Data Management and Database Technology
Systems Design and Documentation
The IBM 5100 Portable Computer
Fortran 77
The Standard Data Encryption Algorithm
Introduction to Distributed Data Processing
Distributed Information Systems
Invitation to Pascal
Invitation to Forth
Microcomputer Graphics and Programming Techniques
Invitation to Ada
Invitation to Ada and Ada Reference Manual
Invitation to Mapper

Operating Systems (2nd Edition)
Local Area Networks
Invitation to MVS (with D. Tharayil)
Introduction to computers and Data Processing
Privacy, Identity, and Cloud Computing

Business and Management

Multinational Computer Systems
Office Automation
Management Support Systems
A Manager's Guide to Productivity, Quality Circles, and
Industrial Robots
Quality Circle Management
Service and Advanced Technology

Basic Research

Managing Uncertainty
Microprogramming Primer

Service Science

A Manager's Guide to Service Science
Foundations of Service Science
Service Science
Introduction to Service
Service Concepts for Management
A Collection of Service Essays
Hospitality and Service

Little Books

The Little Book of Artificial Intelligence
The Little Book of Service Management
The Little Book of Cybersecurity
The Little Book of Cloud Computing
The Little Book of Managing Uncertainty

Novels

The Mysterious Case of the Royal Baby
The Curious Case of the Royal Marriage
The Auspicious Case of the General and the Royal Family
A Case of Espionage
Shelter in Place
The Virus
The Pandemic
Life is Good
The Vaccine
A Tale of Discovery
The Terrorist Plot
An Untimely Situation
The Final Escape
Everything is Good
The Last Adventure
The Romeo Affair
Another Romeo Affair
UP, Down and Anywhere (Duology)
We Can Only HOPE for It

<<<<<<<<<<<>>>>>>>>>>>

Reprints

The Royal Baby
The Royal Marriage
The General and Royal Family
Espionage in Academia
A Shelter is Good
Pandemic Story
The Good Life
The Discovery
The Terrorists
An Unexpected Happening
Service Management
Cybersecurity
Managing Uncertainty
Here, There and Everywhere
Retired Old Men Eating Out, Vols. One and Two

Advanced Novels

The Day After the Night Before
The Journey of Matt and the General
Two Necessary Escapes
Escape

Trilogies and Duologies

The Magnificent Monarchy
Worldwide Trouble
Winning is Good
The Good Life and Discovery

END OF BOOKS BY HARRY KATZAN JR.